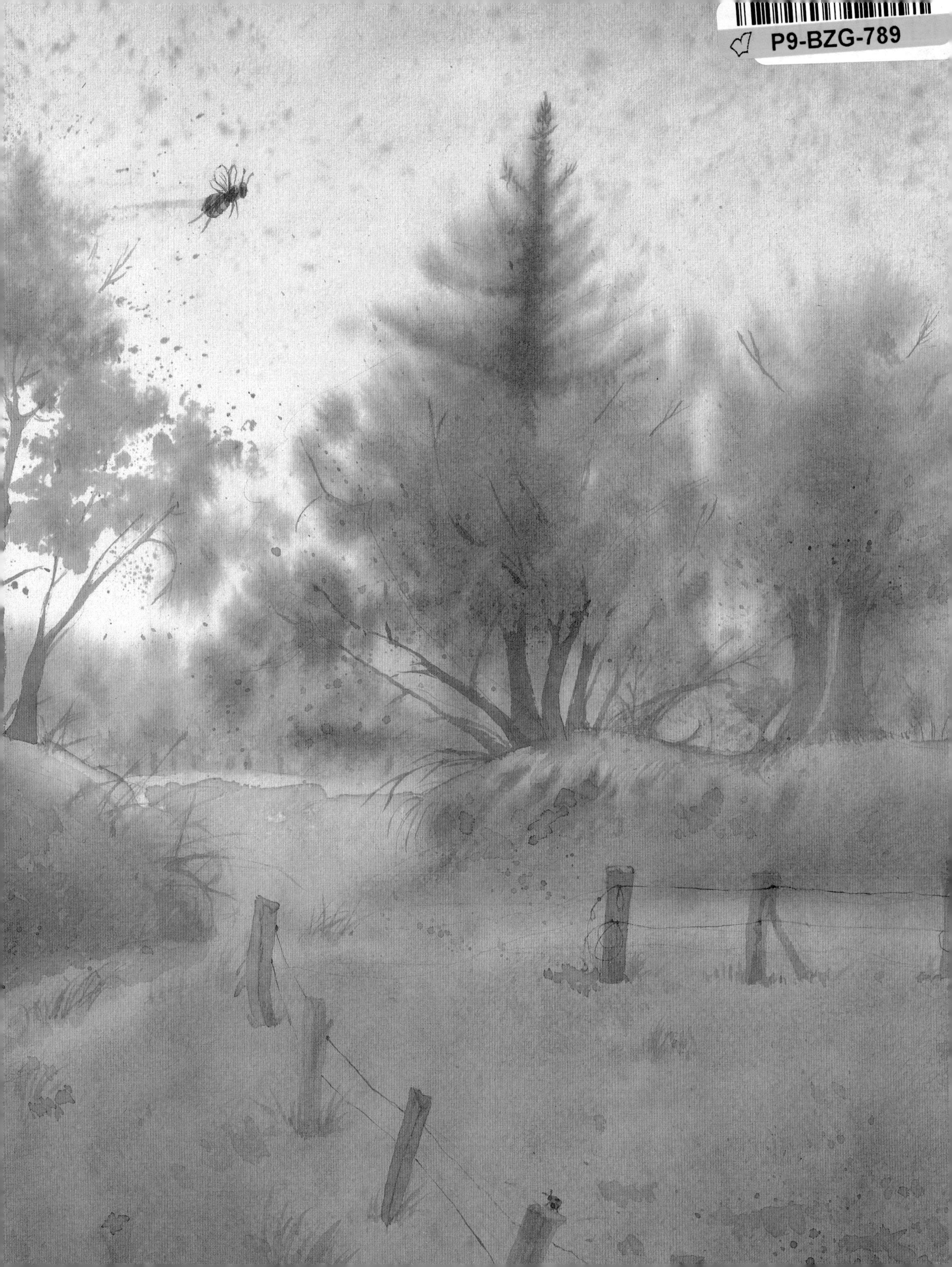

MR. BADGER AND MRS. FOX #3

WHAT A TEAM!

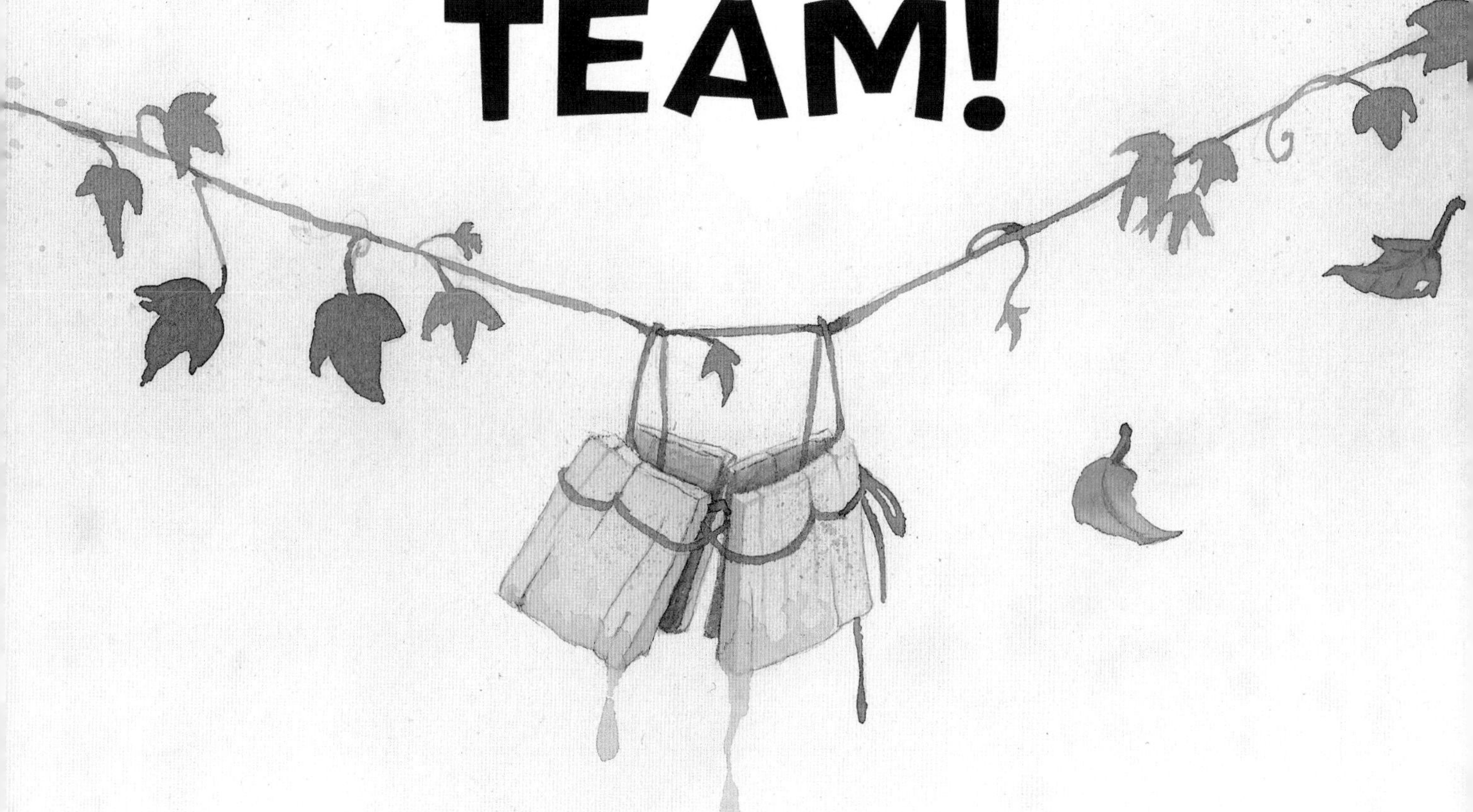

Brigitte LUCIANI & Eve THARLET

Graphic Universe™ • Minneapolis • New York • London

For Christian, Brigitte, Marguerite, and Edmond
for the escape they gave me...
—E.T.

Story by Brigitte Luciani

Art by Eve Tharlet

Translation by Edward Gauvin

First American edition published in 2011 by Graphic Universe™.
Published by arrangement with MEDIATOON LICENSING - France.

Monsieur Blaireau et Madame Renarde
3/Quelle équipe!
© DARGAUD 2009 - Tharlet & Luciani
www.dargaud.com

Graphic Universe™
A division of Lerner Publishing Group, Inc.
241 First Avenue North
Minneapolis, MN 55401 U.S.A.

Website address: www.lernerbooks.com

Library of Congress Cataloging-in-Publication Data available.

ISBN: 978-0-7613-5627-1

Manufactured in the United States of America
1 - DP - 12/31/10

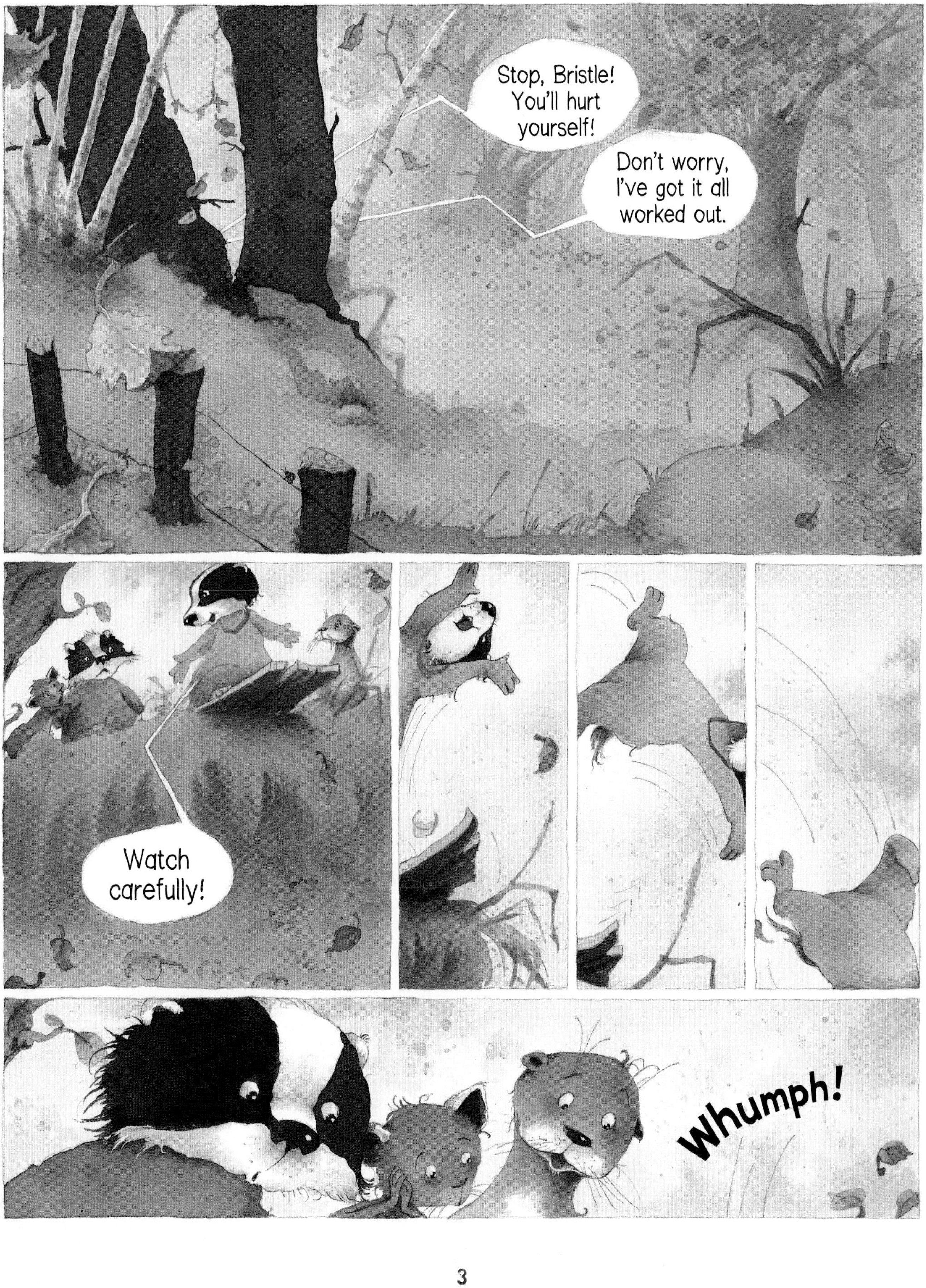
Stop, Bristle! You'll hurt yourself!
Don't worry, I've got it all worked out.
Watch carefully!
Whumph!

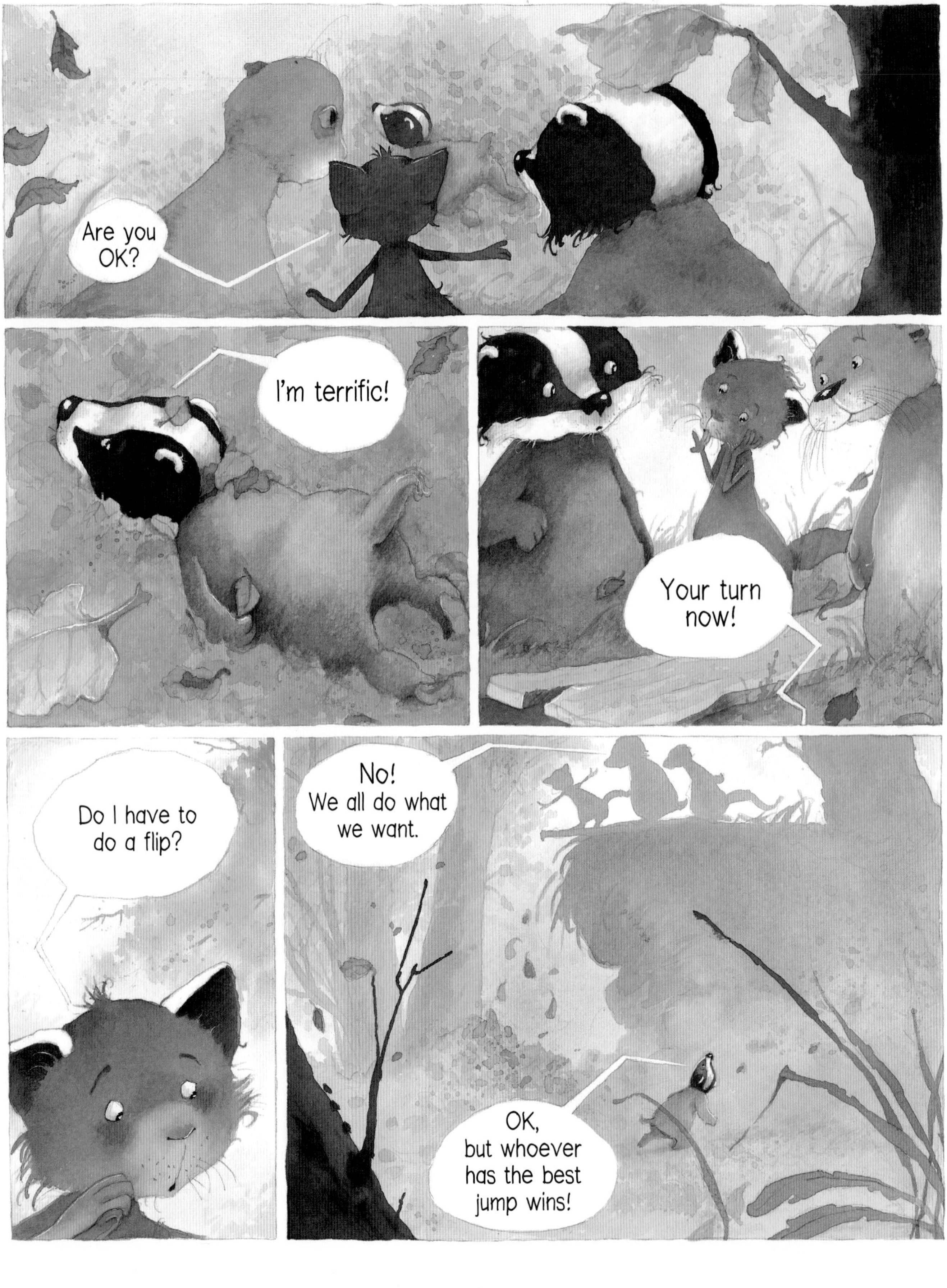
Are you OK?
I'm terrific!
Your turn now!
Do I have to do a flip?
No! We all do what we want.
OK, but whoever has the best jump wins!

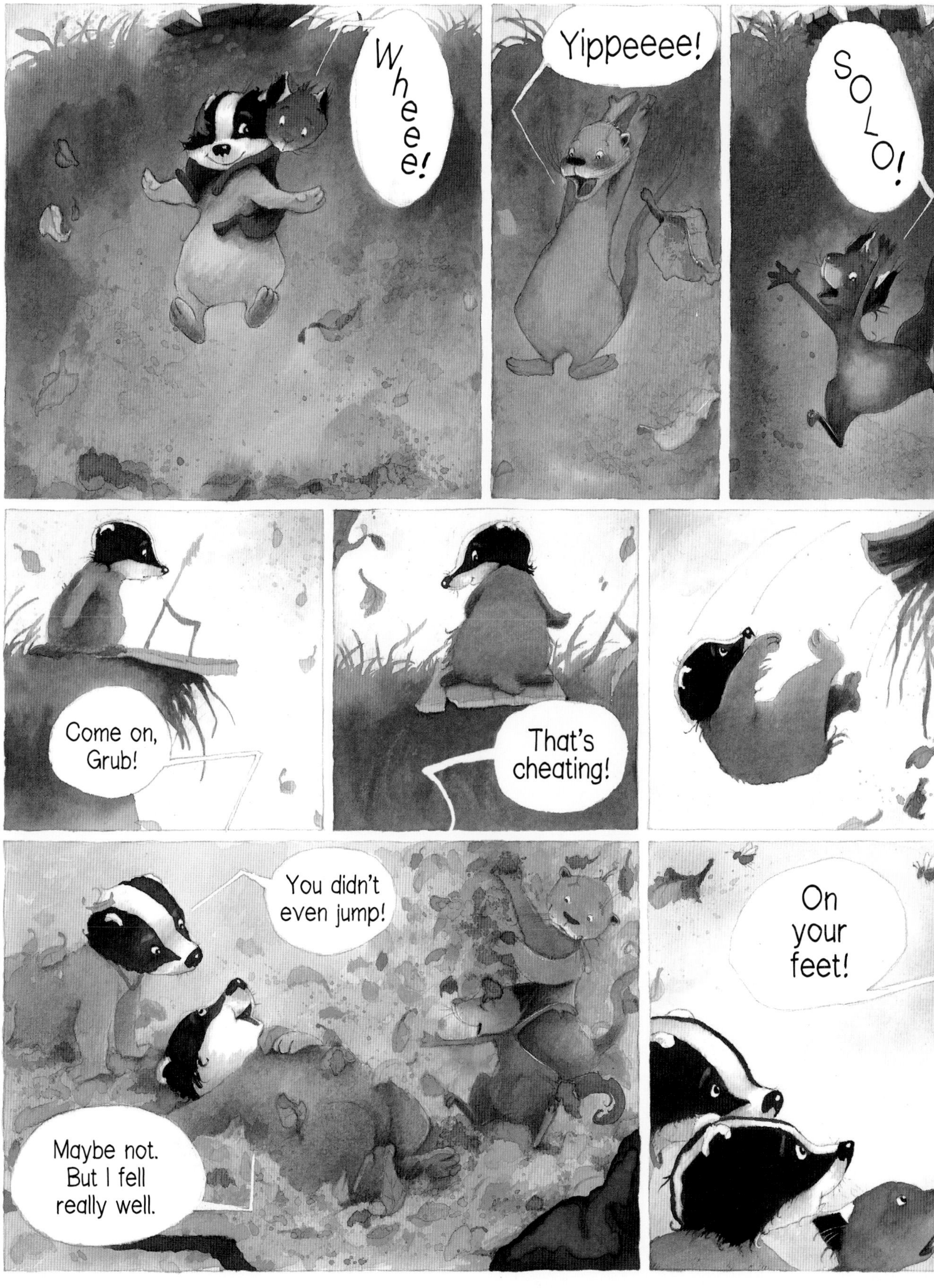
Wheee!
Yippeeee!
SOLO!
Come on, Grub!
That's cheating!
You didn't even jump!
Maybe not. But I fell really well.
On your feet!

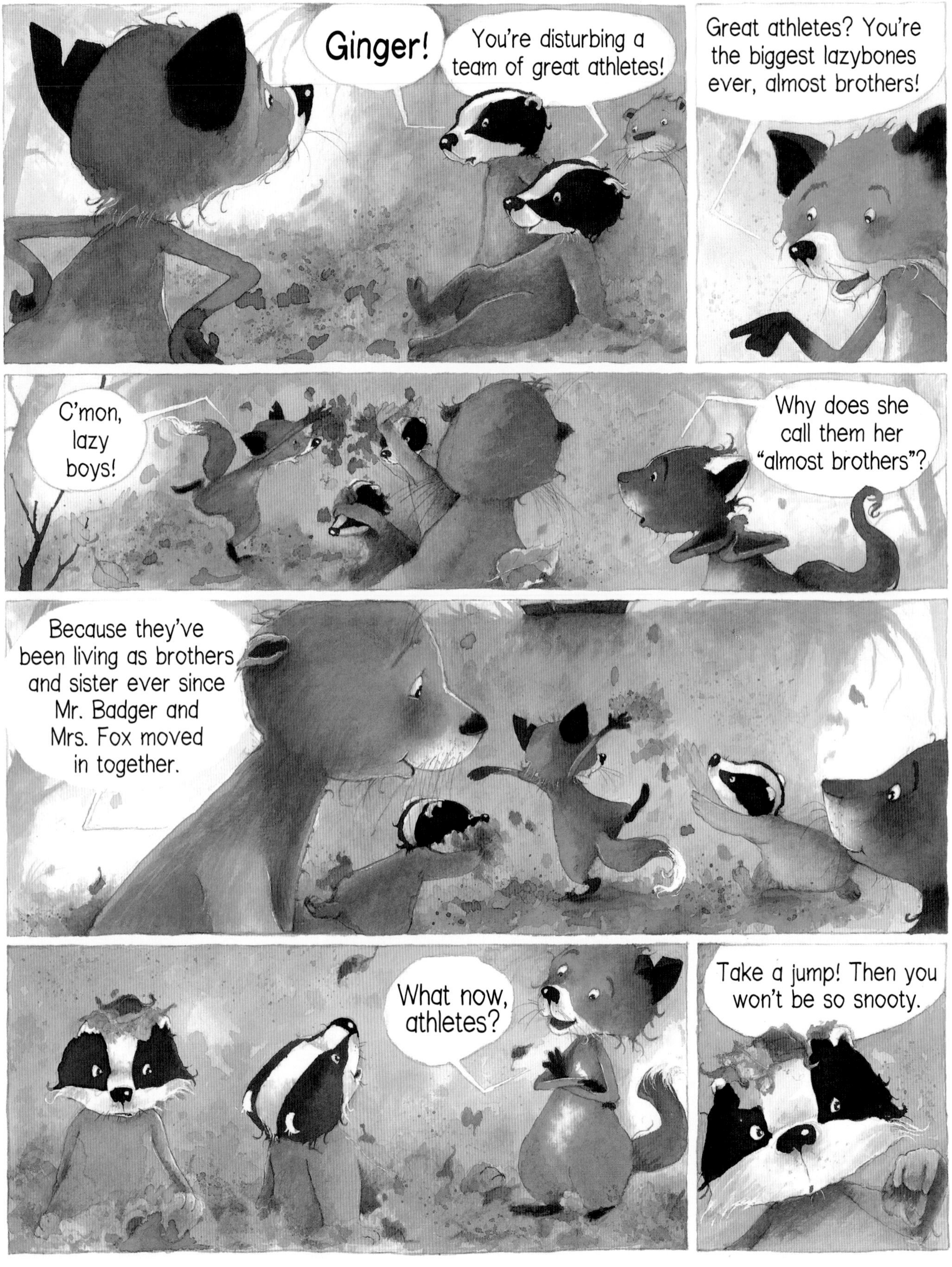
Ginger!
You're disturbing a team of great athletes!
Great athletes? You're the biggest lazybones ever, almost brothers!
C'mon, lazy boys!
Why does she call them her "almost brothers"?
Because they've been living as brothers and sister ever since Mr. Badger and Mrs. Fox moved in together.
What now, athletes?
Take a jump! Then you won't be so snooty.

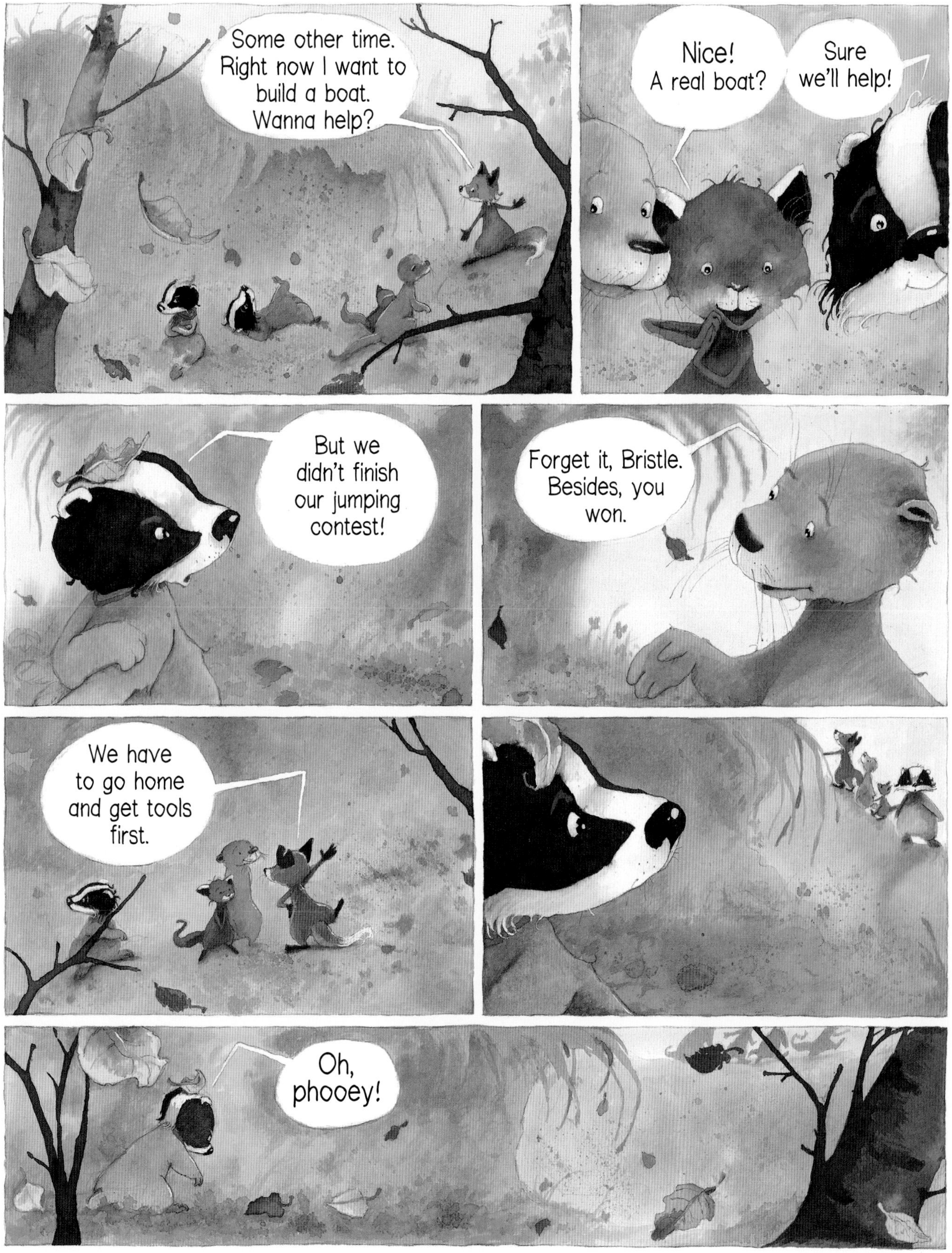
Some other time. Right now I want to build a boat. Wanna help?
Nice! A real boat?
Sure we'll help!
But we didn't finish our jumping contest!
Forget it, Bristle. Besides, you won.
We have to go home and get tools first.
Oh, phooey!

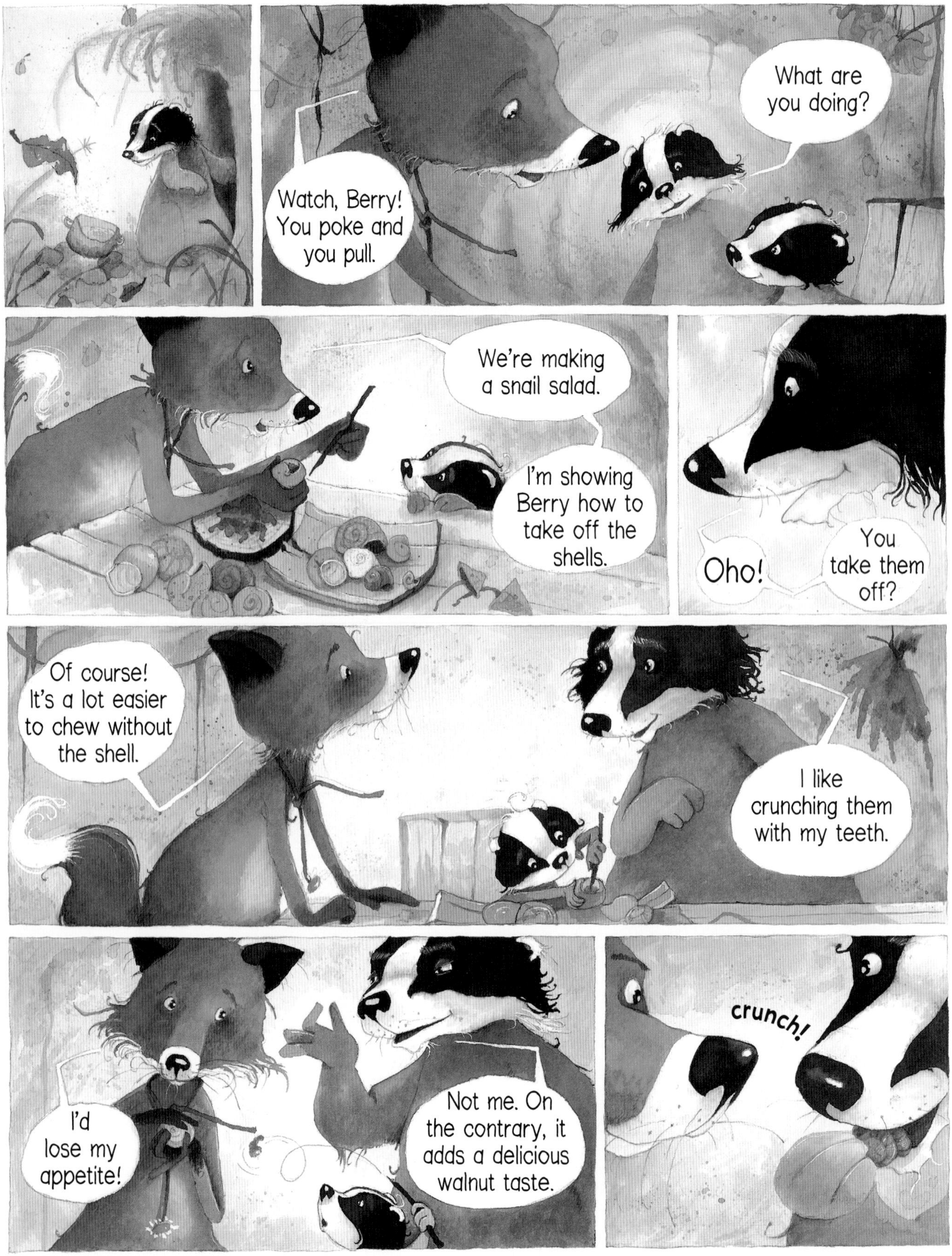
What are you doing?
Watch, Berry! You poke and you pull.
We're making a snail salad.
I'm showing Berry how to take off the shells.
Oho!
You take them off?
Of course! It's a lot easier to chew without the shell.
I like crunching them with my teeth.
I'd lose my appetite!
Not me. On the contrary, it adds a delicious walnut taste.
crunch!

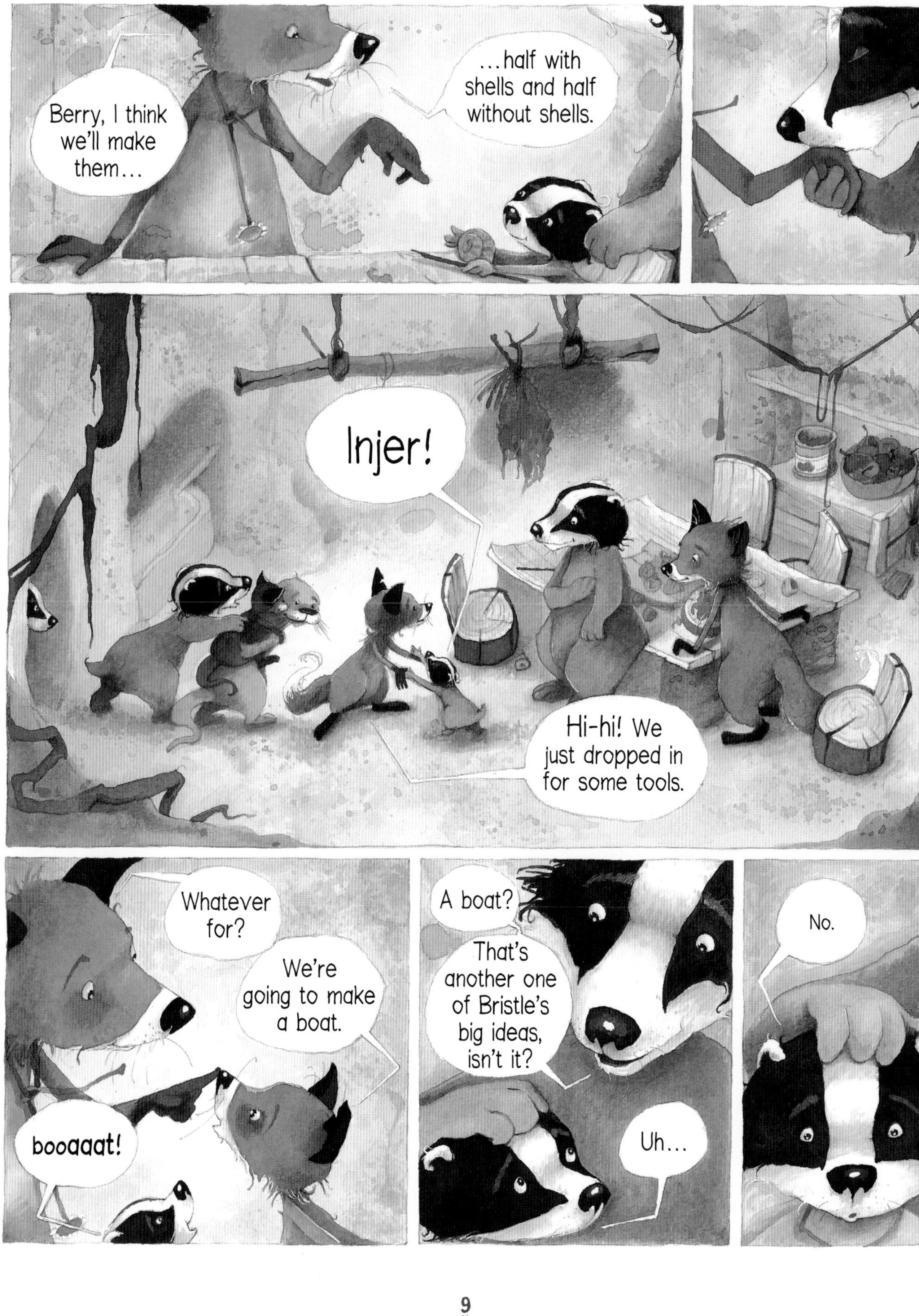
Berry, I think we'll make them...
...half with shells and half without shells.
Injer!
Hi-hi! We just dropped in for some tools.
Whatever for?
We're going to make a boat.
booaaat!
A boat?
That's another one of Bristle's big ideas, isn't it?
Uh...
No.

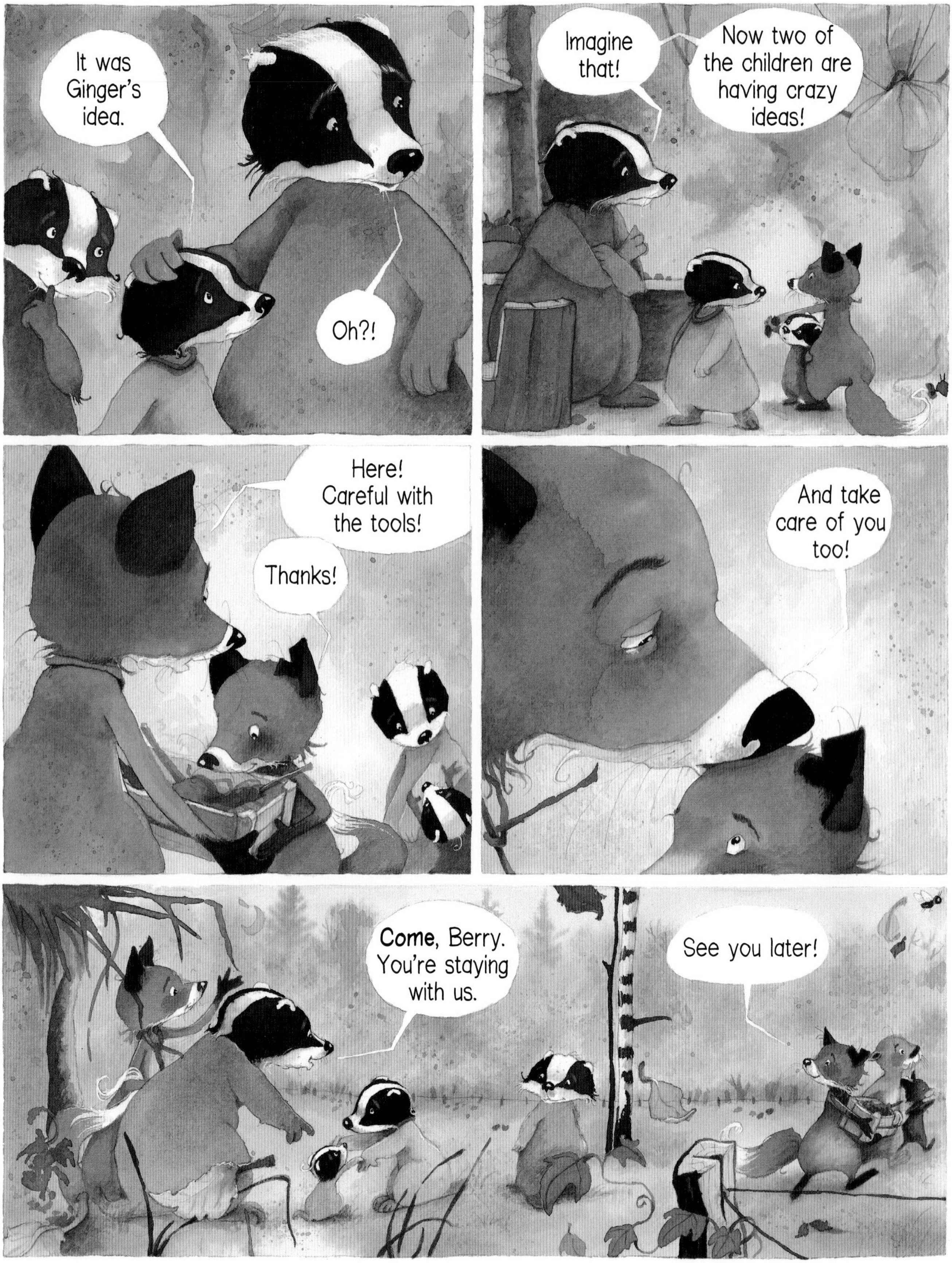
It was Ginger's idea.
Oh?!
Imagine that!
Now two of the children are having crazy ideas!
Here! Careful with the tools!
Thanks!
And take care of you too!
Come, Berry. You're staying with us.
See you later!

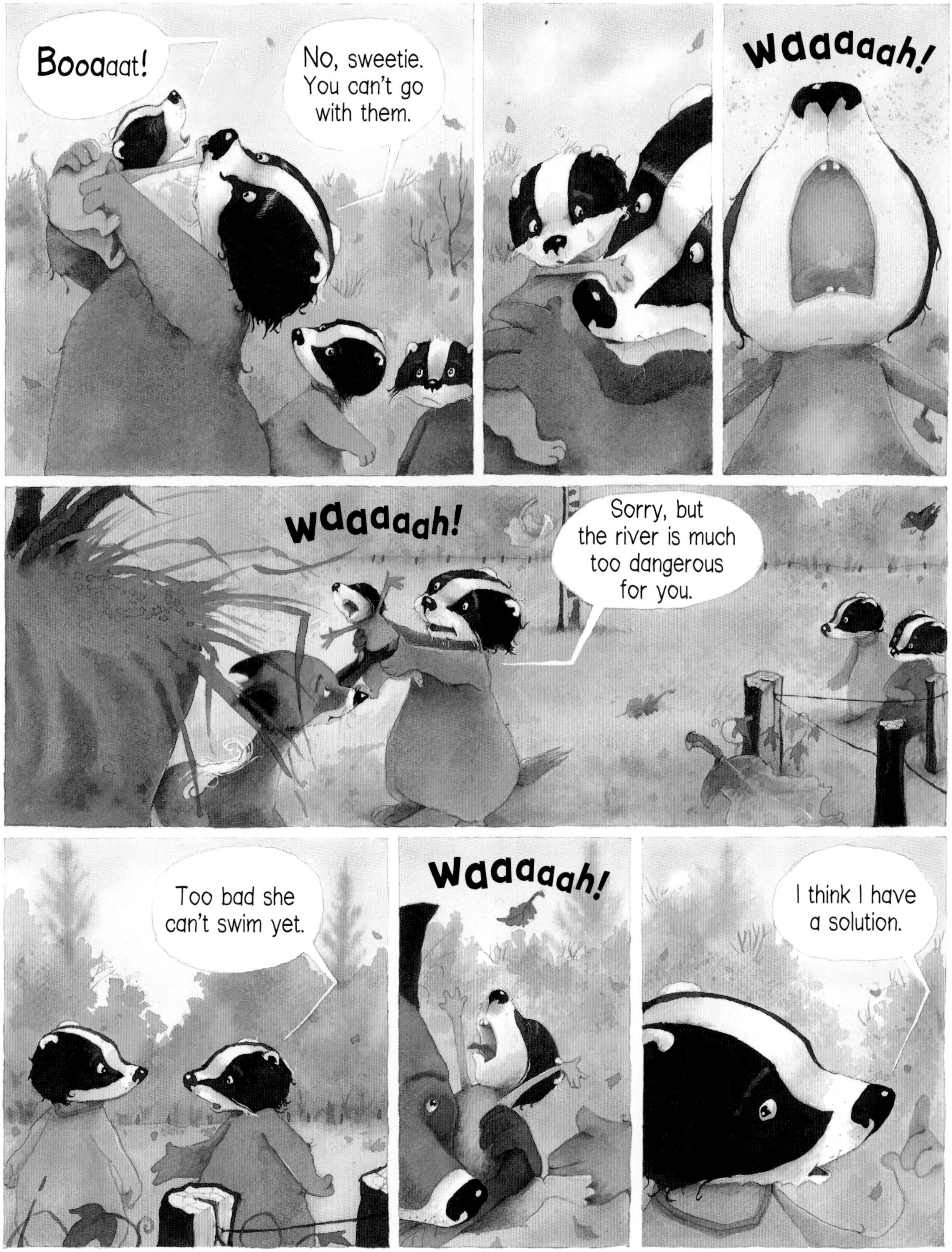
Booaaat!
No, sweetie. You can't go with them.
Waaaaah!
Waaaaah!
Sorry, but the river is much too dangerous for you.
Too bad she can't swim yet.
Waaaaah!
I think I have a solution.

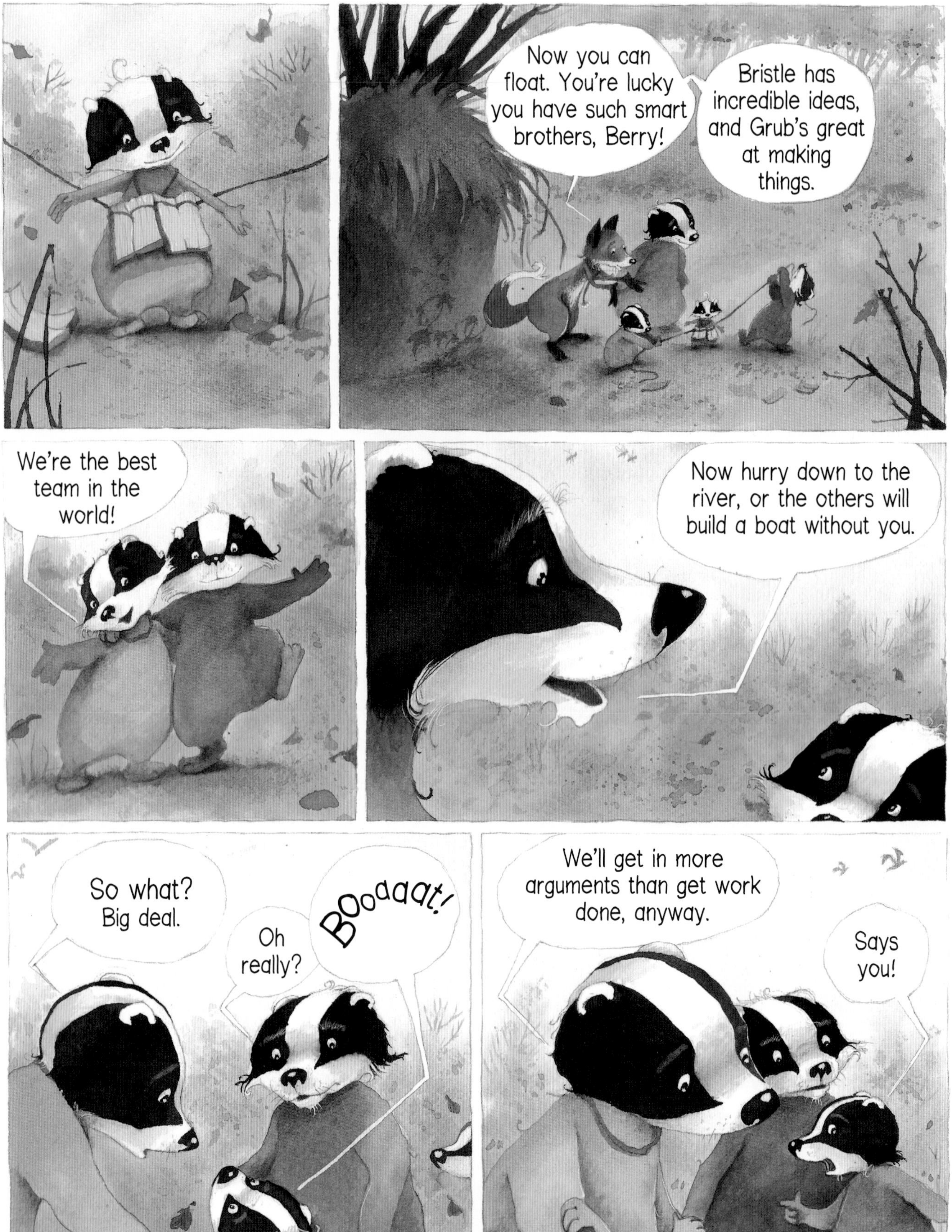
Now you can float. You're lucky you have such smart brothers, Berry!
Bristle has incredible ideas, and Grub's great at making things.
We're the best team in the world!
Now hurry down to the river, or the others will build a boat without you.
So what? Big deal.
Oh really?
BOoaaat!
We'll get in more arguments than get work done, anyway.
Says you!

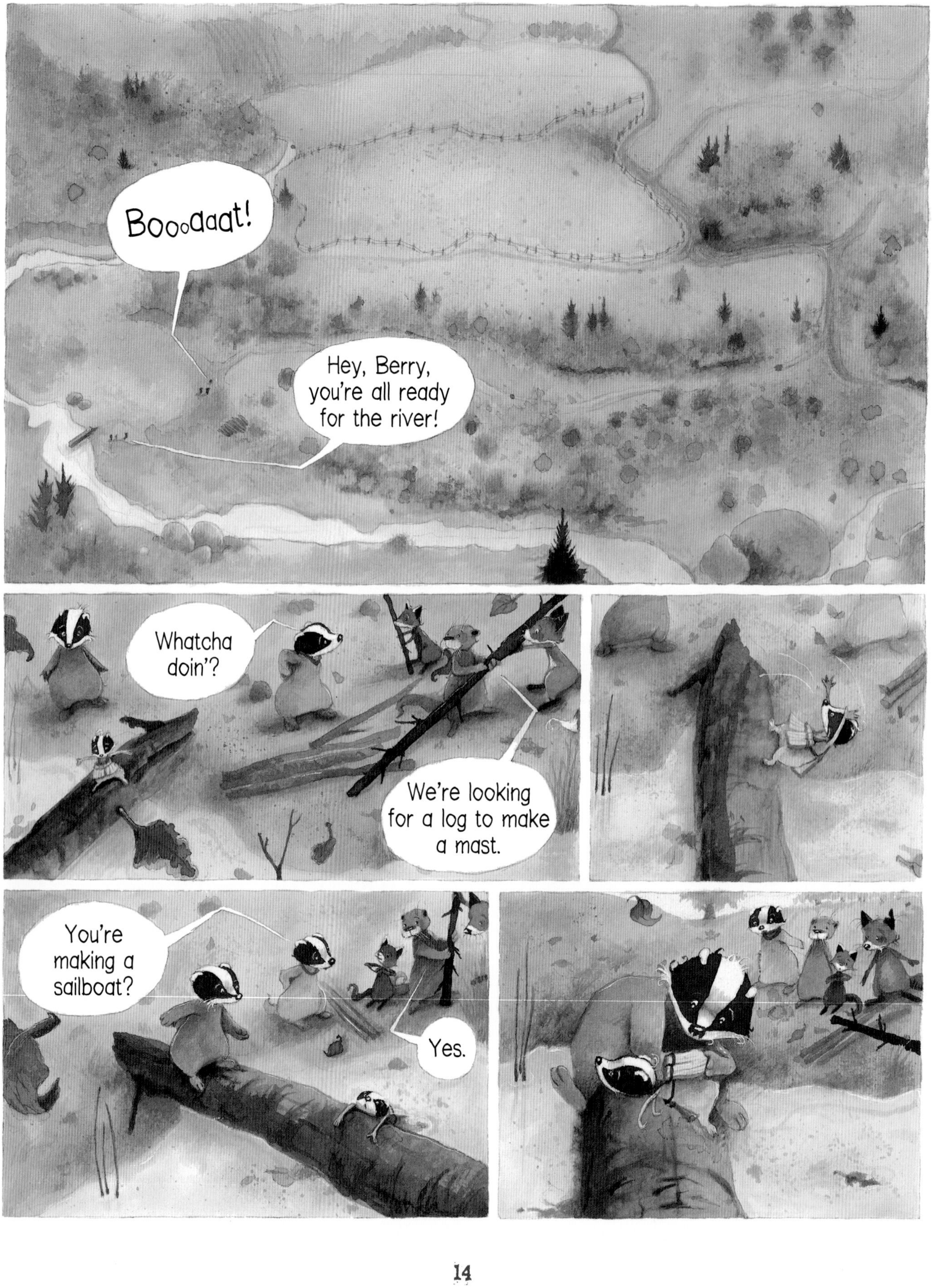
Booooaaat!
Hey, Berry, you're all ready for the river!
Whatcha doin'?
We're looking for a log to make a mast.
You're making a sailboat?
Yes.

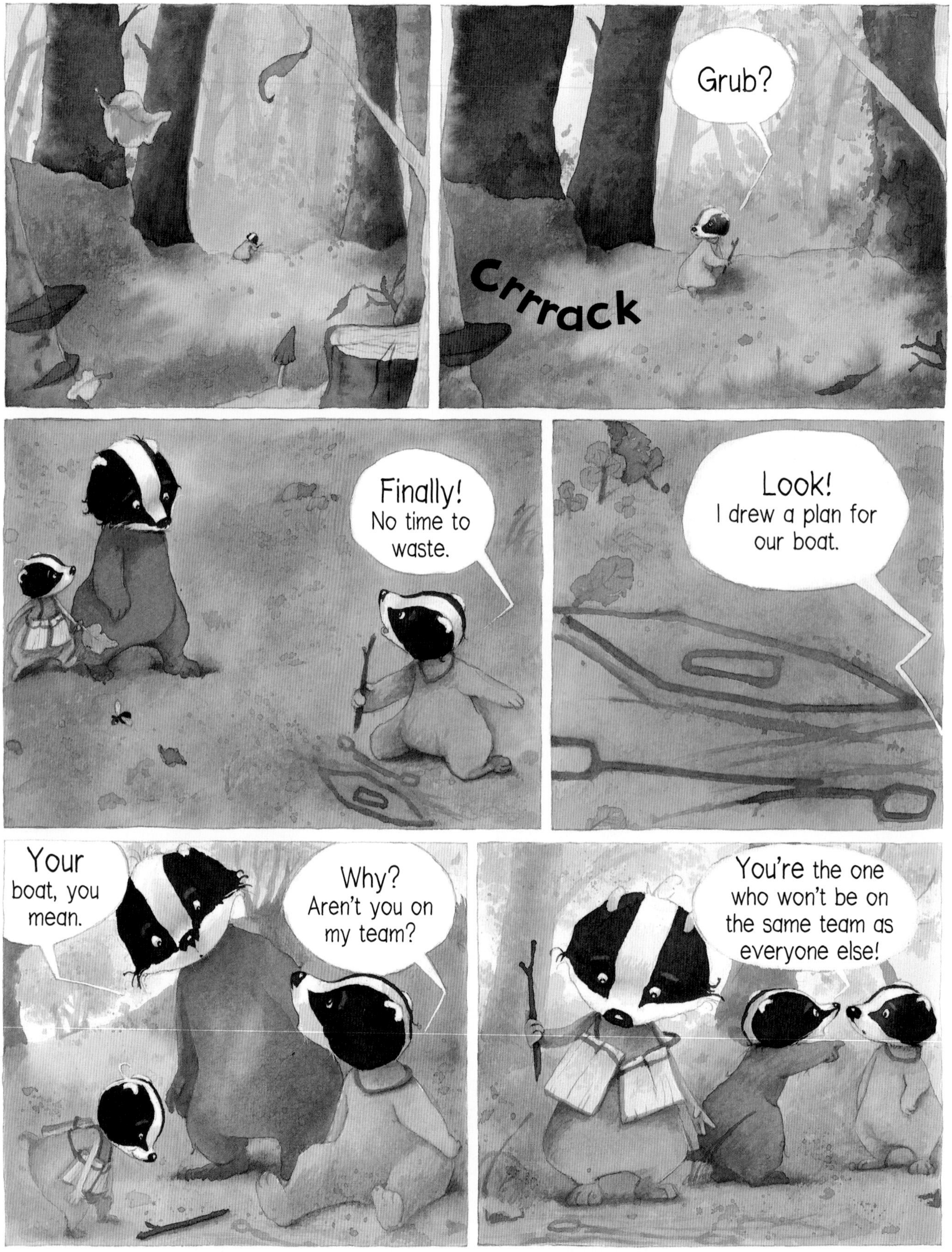
Grub?
Crrrack
Finally! No time to waste.
Look! I drew a plan for our boat.
Your boat, you mean.
Why? Aren't you on my team?
You're the one who won't be on the same team as everyone else!

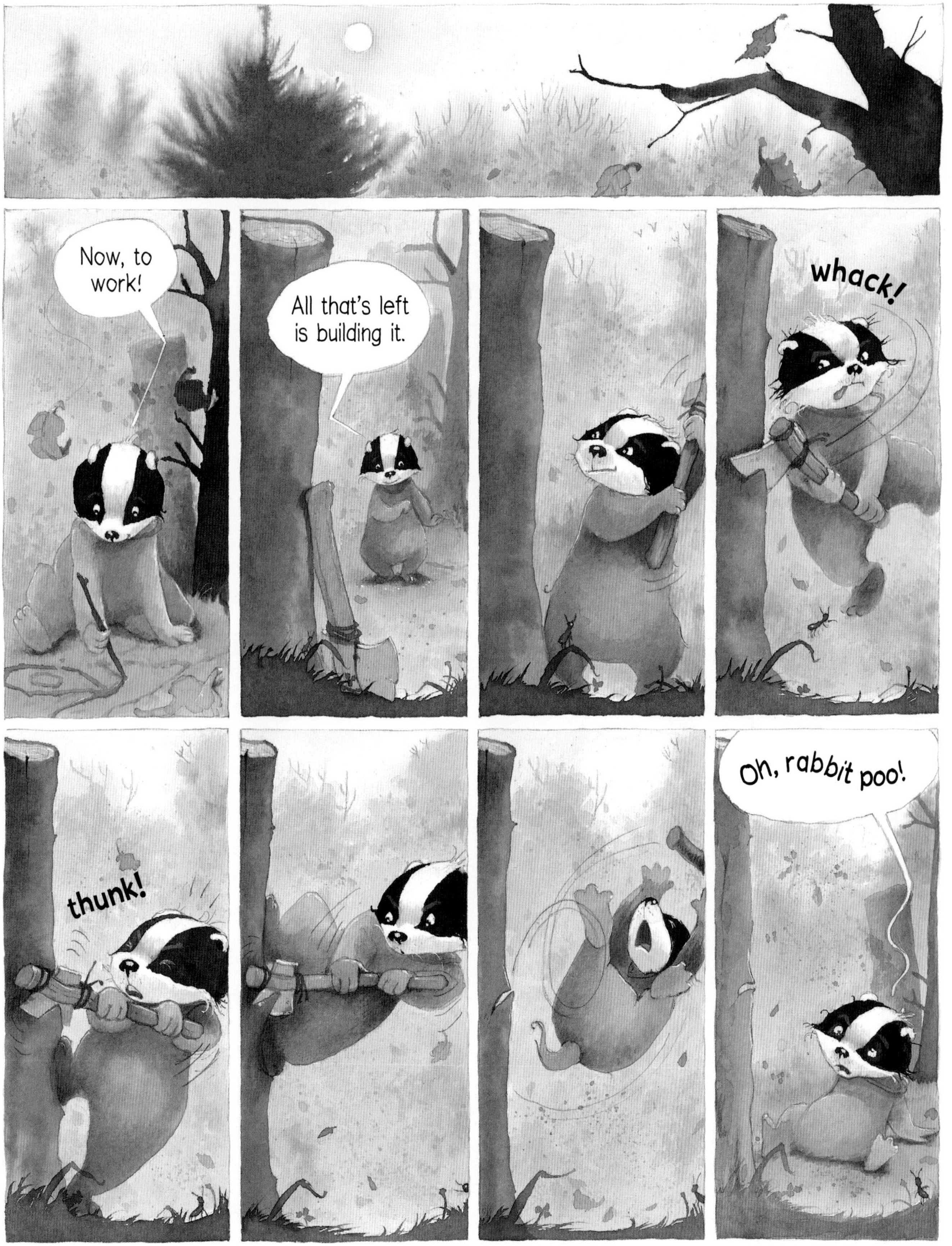
Now, to work!
All that's left is building it.
whack!
thunk!
Oh, rabbit poo!

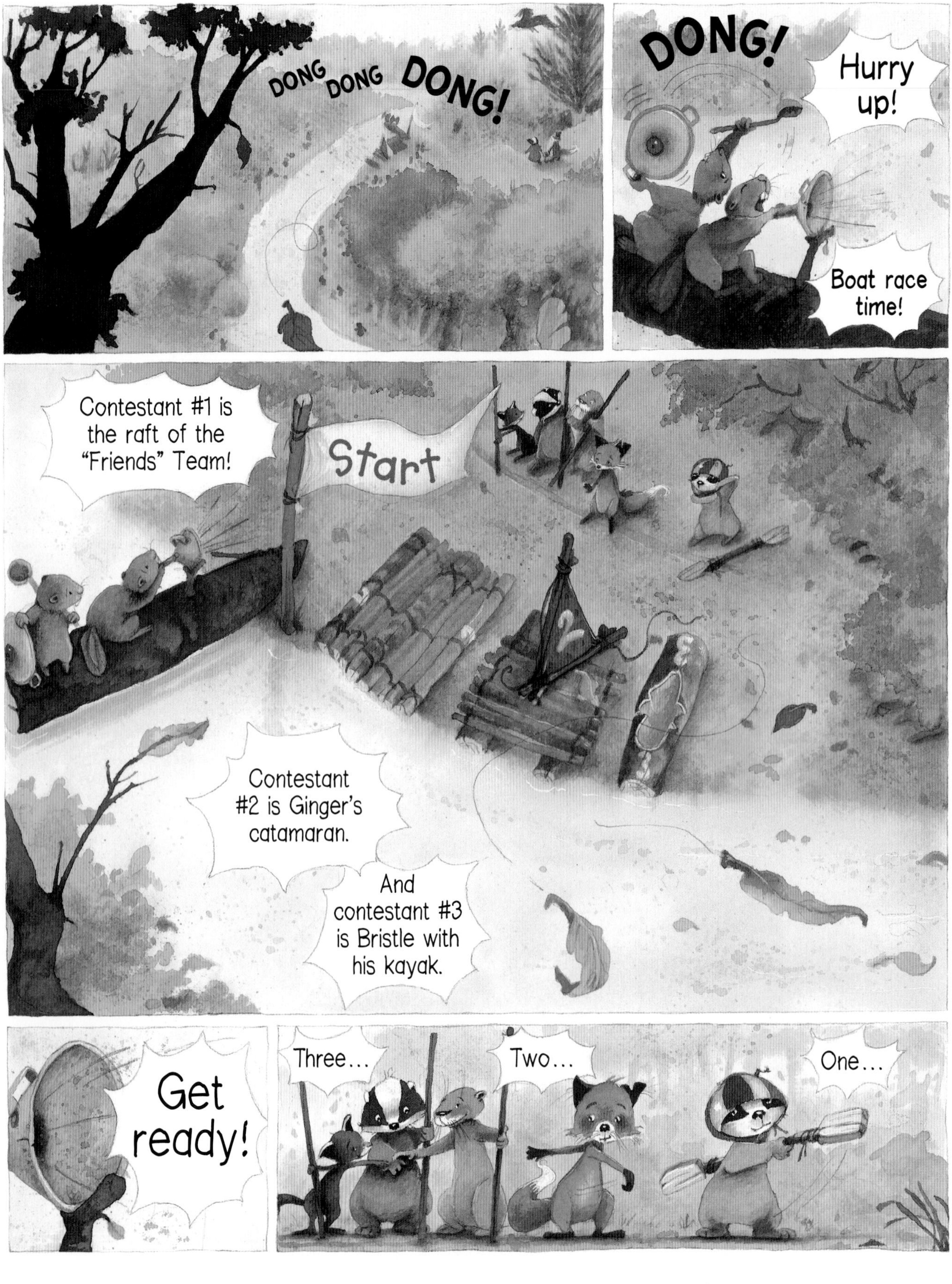
DONG DONG DONG!
DONG!
Hurry up!
Boat race time!
Contestant #1 is the raft of the "Friends" Team!
Start
Contestant #2 is Ginger's catamaran.
And contestant #3 is Bristle with his kayak.
Get ready!
Three...
Two...
One...

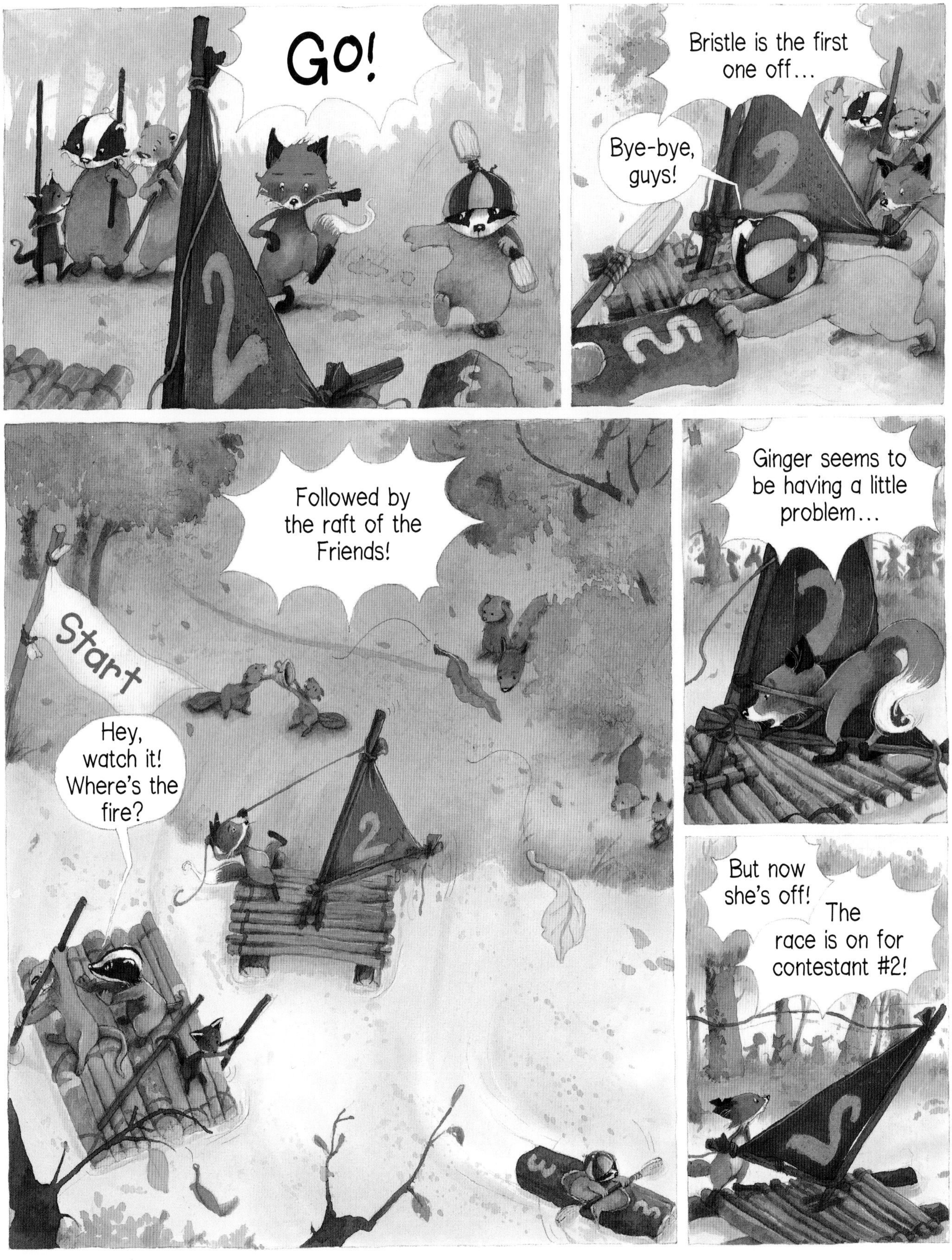
GO!
Bristle is the first one off...
Bye-bye, guys!
Followed by the raft of the Friends!
Start
Hey, watch it! Where's the fire?
Ginger seems to be having a little problem...
But now she's off!
The race is on for contestant #2!

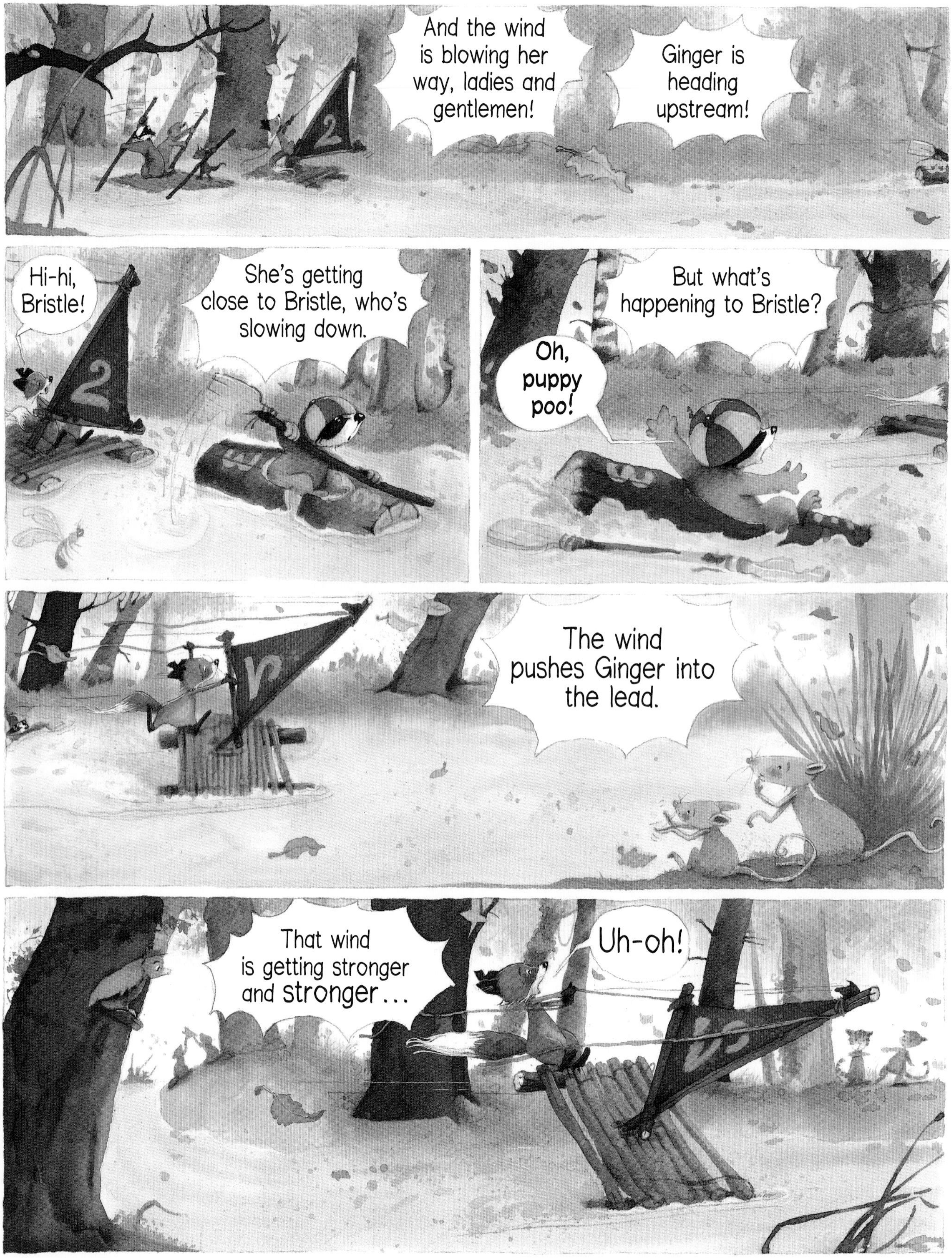
And the wind is blowing her way, ladies and gentlemen!
Ginger is heading upstream!
Hi-hi, Bristle!
She's getting close to Bristle, who's slowing down.
But what's happening to Bristle?
Oh, puppy poo!
The wind pushes Ginger into the lead.
That wind is getting stronger and stronger...
Uh-oh!

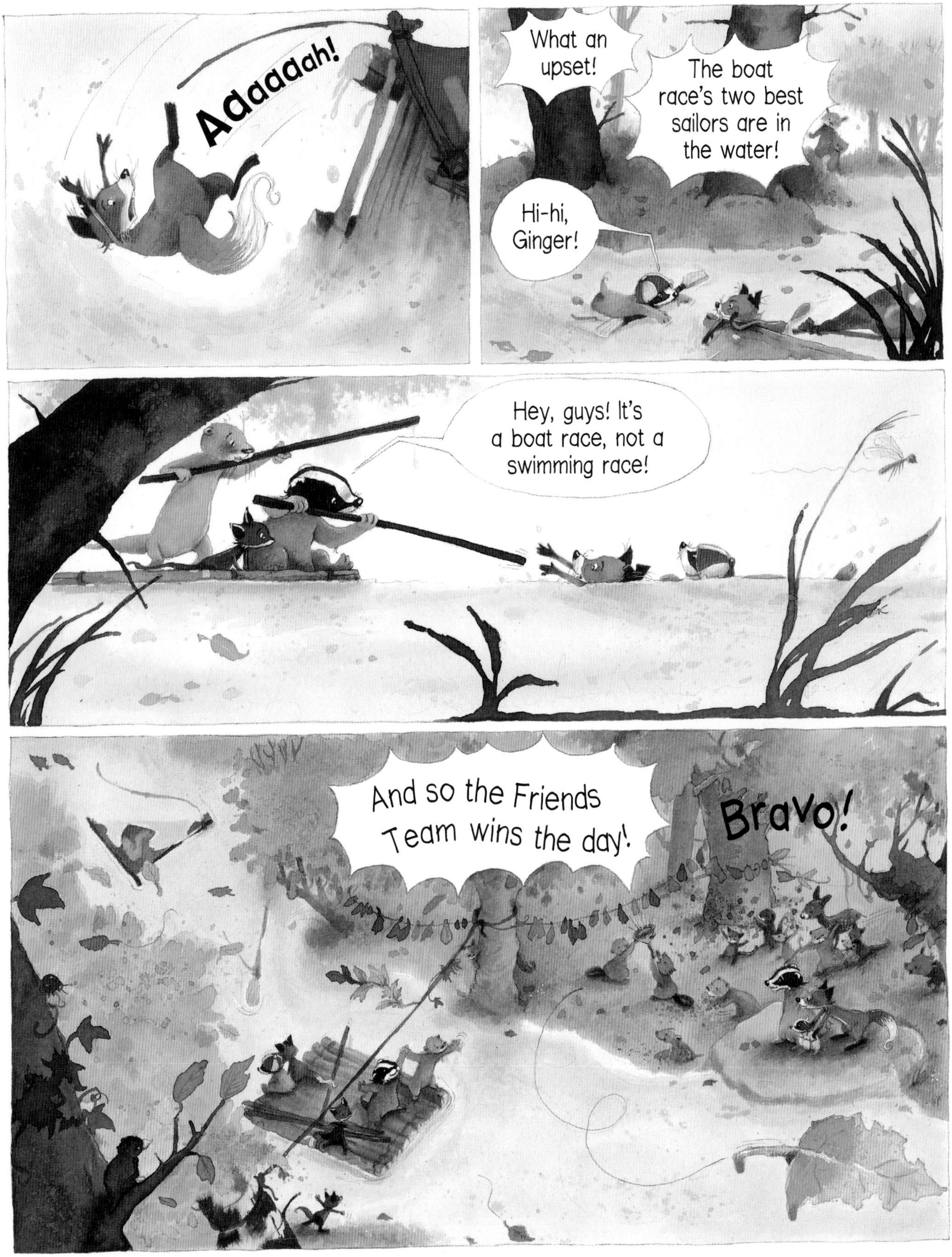
Aaaaaah!
What an upset!
The boat race's two best sailors are in the water!
Hi-hi, Ginger!
Hey, guys! It's a boat race, not a swimming race!
And so the Friends Team wins the day!
Bravo!

31

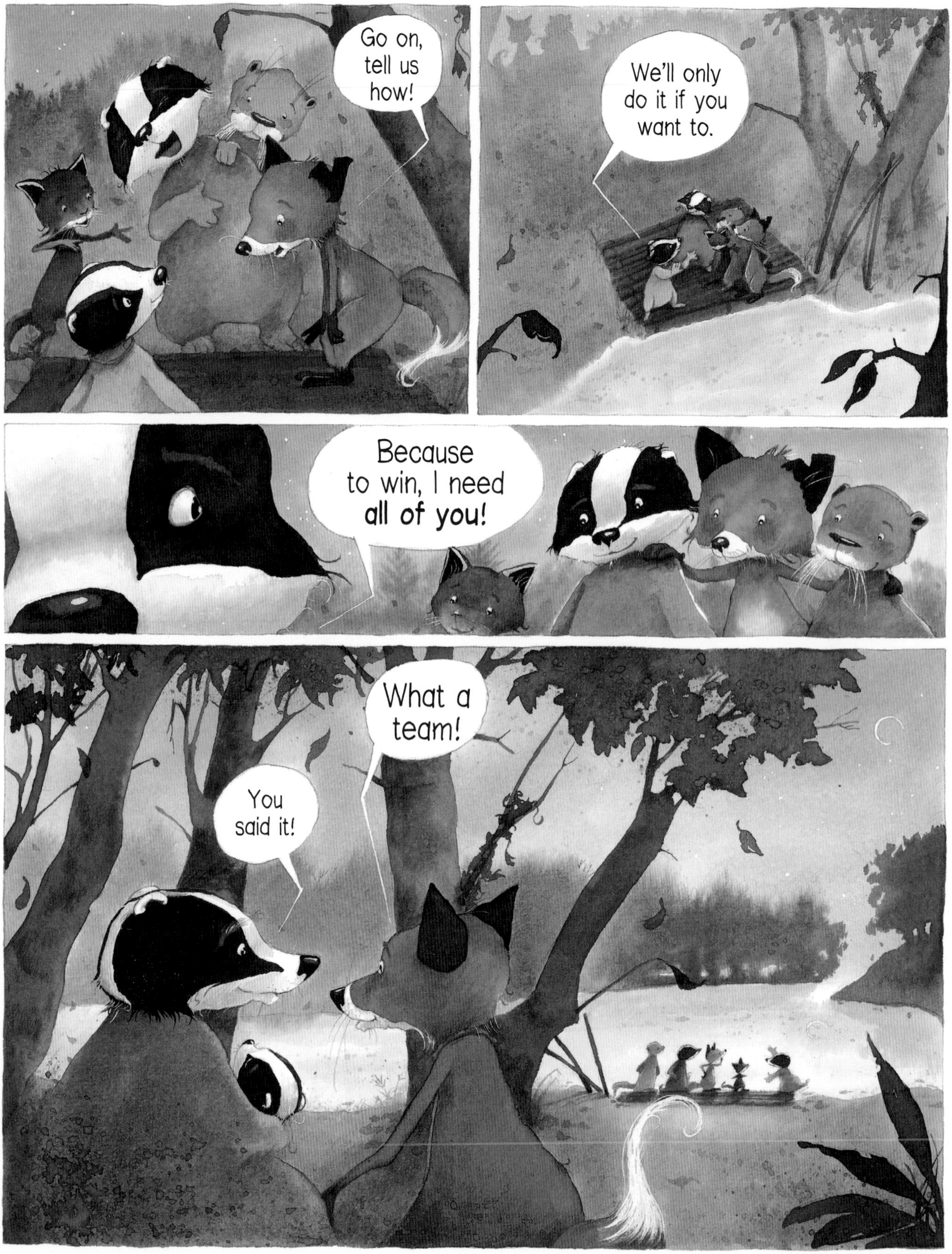
Go on, tell us how!
We'll only do it if you want to.
Because to win, I need **all of you!**
What a team!
You said it!